VIRGO
AUGUST 23 – SEPTEMBER 22

baby

Look out, world!

A Virgo was born on _____.

What is my Virgo Baby destined to be?

You'll take things as they come.

You'll move at an unhurried pace.

Everything blooms when it's supposed to. Life is not a race.

Do you know you are an earth sign?

You know how to stay

calm, grounded, and steady.

You may need to be a hermit sometimes.

You'll open up when you're ready.

Do you have an adventure planned for today?

Let's check your list!

You always find beauty in the details.

You're known for being a perfectionist.

You are a down-to-earth soul

with such a playful heart.

Others will be able to depend on you.

You're tremendously loyal from the start.

You have a creative mind.

I know you will design a life that you adore.

Sweet dreams, sweet Virgo.

I hope you grow up to get everything you want plus more.

About the Author

Jen Neary is a Sagittarius who always felt like she was destined to be a writer. As the only fire sign in her family, she was inspired to create this modern zodiac baby book series for parents and guardians to learn more about their child's character traits and unique greatness.

Printed in the USA
CPSIA information can be obtained
at www.ICGtesting.com
LVHW060843250923
757900LV00004BA/32